I0556916

The Gilford Collection

A Series of Unimportant Moments
By Caleb D. McFarland

The Gilford Collection

Introduction

The first story I wrote, when I was around thirteen, started with a man looking at his shadow on a wall. He sat in a dimly lit room, thinking. The story was about a half-alien who owned a detective agency that looked into cases to do with paranormal things. You could say that I was a seat of the pants type writer, meaning I didn't plan, I just wrote. Many of the stories survive, some were probably lost. Someday I will probably come upon some of those first printed pages, the first of my creations. What would come to be after that, through whatever idea popped into my head, is a story about aliens, half aliens, secret powers, and a good deal of walking down long hallways with doors shaking from blue, pulsating energy at the end. To the best of my knowledge none of my stories we very good then. They were creative, well imagined scenes that came to me like dream sequences, with no other creative basis for writing them other than I liked the idea of what I was describing. If it didn't work as a story, I didn't care. I just liked to write and imagine things. I liked creating with anything I could. But as I got older, I changed and my stories and my creative side changed with me. This was both good and bad. When I was younger it was easier to write, but as I have grown I have become more critical of what my work 'should be'. I am a better writer now, but writing is sometimes harder. One thing that made it fun as a kid was a talent for description; I always knew how I wanted to describe something, that aspect came naturally to me. And I wasn't bad at creating an interesting story, but my ability to structure that story was not as strong. (I was centered mostly around science fiction, fantasy, and thrillers then.) I didn't have enough craft to turn my skill into something more developed. In the beginning, creatives are inconsistently good. They only have half of the equation. Craft allows them to connect to their skill, to wield it like a tool. These stories mark the beginning and continued development of my craft. As I have studied and written, I have become more able to create a solid story while expressing what I mean. The evolution of my thought and craft is shown in this little collection. It is like a timeline.

If you are human, you are a

storyteller. Our thoughts are guided by the narrative in our head. Our experience in life is dependent on the story we tell ourselves. So story is more important than many may think. A story is more than a drama, a comedy, or a thriller. Our unique story is our unique way of life.

A story is also powerful, because changing the story you tell yourself changes the life you experience. And through every story we hear our story is influenced. From the vast array of details to the plot points of major life events, every sight and sound is filtered through our inner narrative. It decides for us what is important in our lives. It guides us. Our stories are all powerful over us. Without them we would be lost in a world of choice, no point of reference to guide us. A lot of the time our story does not align with reality. It is like a self created matrix, where good and bad are defined by our values, our programming.

If you would have asked me what my first story was about, I would have tried to explain my vague thoughts. And though I had a lot to learn by the way of craft, process, and the deeper matters of why I really wanted to write, I had two of the most important things in the undertaking of anything: desire and creativity. I would keep moving forward and learning because I wanted to, and I could apply that education effectively with my imagination. My work was built upon apparitions of my imagination. Simple things tell simple stories. But as I have grown, so have my interests, my concerns. So though I started with a simple desire to create good stories, and though that desire remains, something else has taken up residence in my mind. Concerns. I try to relieve these concerns through writing, and that is where the themes come from. I try to solve some of the bigger problems that I, and many others, face through one of the most powerful tools humans possess: story.

The big can be seen and understood through the small parts of our lives, through the little symbols we create in our minds. It was all there, all the secrets of life, in the small things, hidden in plain sight. It is about the deception of where the important things lie. It is about your small thought being as important as the stars. Because all things, all the big concepts, philosophies, and questions, can be understood through the small thing, the stone lion or the broken boat. Though I had many ideas on what it is I was saying while writing these stories, this is the one idea that best defines my purpose. You can sense it more in some stories than in others, but it is in all of them to some degree.

In some ways, I have moved far from that man in a room. In other ways, I am doing the same things differently. My people, my characters, have never stopped thinking, just as I have not. They keep trying to get to something, to understand something, they all, each of them in their own way, are grasping at something. They seek to understand life, to gather up these wisdoms and build something better. Even more basic than the search for a better, truer life, is the search for peace, for a level of existence that is closer to right, that allows us to gain understanding without losing peace, that allows us to live in spite of our doubts, or maybe because of them. Characters inherit the demons of their creators, and mine our my doubts. So I search through them, for a way to live with uncertainty, for a way to be smart without being too smart for our own good.

The lives of these people are threatened by what it is they want, their 'own good' or well being is taken from them when they come upon the realization that they cannot move forward without an answer to something that bothers them. They are threatened from within, by a crisis of philosophy, an ultimatum of view points. The question to ask of these stories is: do the individuals find their answers, or do they learn to live because of their questions. Does it become a detractor or a motivator. What does their nature do to them, to their lives.

In these stories, in these moments, we seek for the happy medium of life. To know and to not be disturbed by that knowing. It seems that before life we hide in ignorance, but after life has come, we mourn the loss of innocence. No happy medium it seems. But within the noise, within the unimportant, there is a spark, and that spark means more than the fire. For without it, there would be no fire. If we could honor the spark of small things, we would understand the fire that is the nature of the universe.

I have heard that great things have

small beginnings. I hope it is the same with this small book.

Acknowledgments

Thanks to Merrell Palmer for helping me correct some of my repetitive writing mistakes. You make me look smarter, (which should be everyones job if you ask me).

Dedication

I dedicate this book to my grandfather Lowell Edward Ashby, (1934-2014.)

I will miss your smile and I will try to keep your heart. Such rare a treasure cannot become a coin at the bottom of the sea. But it shouldn't be put in a case either. Your's is a treasure that is kept in a worn pocket, that is brought out on rainy days and sunny days a like. Your's is a treasure, a love, for all seasons. And I will treasure it for all seasons, and never forget he who bestowed it upon me.

Table of Contents

Part One

A Dream of Gilford

The Dead Call You By Name

One Immortal Thing

In The Forest

Trees As Prison Guards

The Doctor And The Patient

Walkways of Light

The Death of A Sunrise

Part One

The rain came to wash the village. It had committed no sin, but it had seen conflict in its time. I was taking another street home. My mind was taking many other streets, wandering the cosmos in search of something of substance.

I had read books on writing: understand plot, stakes, how to create a sympathetic character, when to show, when to tell. These concepts were shiny toys thrown at a towering wall.' I did not know myself, and the process of progression I move to. I did not know what I needed."

A Dream of Gilford

The voyage, crew-less except for me, set out from Gilford, a small village in Northern Ireland. My house was between two hills. One of the hills had a long line of trees; cars went up this line of trees and behind the house, trucks with square shapes, like someone was driving boxes up it. And I had heard about a witches' house. I had been told about it by an older boy. He wasn't smart, but I was younger and couldn't help but wonder if he was right about it, and that somewhere in there, there really was a witches house. At night I ran from it in the darkness, like the first dream I ever remembered, where I was running from Batman into my parents room to hide behind their bed.

It was early in the morning, and I set out with

my pounds in my hand. Rubbing my fingers over
the thick, circle pieces. I liked the money. The
coins looked like gold from a treasure chest. I
played with all of the old money I found in the
dim, wooden shelves of the furniture in my
parents room. I managed it. It was a strategy
with me. Everything was. I liked cutting through
a little parking lot and tunnel in a building with
two shops; a tea place and a shop for wedding
dresses, and then you came out just shy of the
circle that was the middle of Gilford. Where at
the end of the day, cars conversed in a dance at
the roundabout, returning home from work. In
the german convenience store that was the Spar
they sold Star Wars pens that fit into a cardboard
pen holder. I had bought a few of them. The
holder was crushed later and lost.

It was like setting out on a long voyage. No
army came with me, only myself. It was a quest
for knowledge, and I headed to some middle

eastern country where books sat on sand colored
shelves and men with beards spoke about art and
philosophy. The day had no sight of rain in it,
and that meant there would be plenty. But what
it is that I couldn't decide, I was still trying to
understand. As I set off down the road, I tried to
remember my dream. I receded from the icy wind
around me to a place that was filled with haunted
darkness; a cold, frightening familiarity flowed
around me. A dark road set before, at its end a
barren playground, one street light above,
reaching slowly out to dimly illuminate the road
and a caravan to the side, an old machine — grey
on green colors, or cream on grey; it was a faded
memory. I pushed up the hill, onto the path by
the woods. The suburbs were on the hill. I knew
kids from there; ruff, small, with their faces
smiling as they tumbled down a hill and got back
up to go again.

I saw at the end of the dim road a child,

25

skinny, with blond hair, blue eyes, squinting into
the light of the street lamp. "Make up your
mind," he said, and began to laugh as he ran onto
the playground to climb the monkey bars, slip
down the slide, and happily swing on the swing
set. He started the process over, alone at play,
happy in the seclusion of his joy. I had no idea
what it meant. I had no idea what anything
meant. I was only here, now, walking to the
library. My goal was simple, I wanted a book. I
felt how tiny the world was, and smiled at my
place far away from it all, being no one. Simple,
easy, wise-inducing, childlike, happy in deliberate
ignorance, I felt these words, and they connected
with me. His name was Child, he stood at the
playground down the road, a perpetual smile
squinting his face. He laughed and began to play.
The rain knew its time; it came. I was soaked by
the time I turned the corner and could see the
little main street of Gilford. The Spar, postoffice,
movie store, Chinese take-out, pot-pie place,

antique store, and the rest, all stood together like the silent mosaic of my childhood. Speak artist, speak, but nothing came that was beyond this place and time, so I walked to the old, two-story library, and sat in the kids' section, reading Eoin Colfer and comic books wrapped in plastic.

"Make up your mind, dear, you have to pay for those books," she said at the desk, "you have to decide: which will you have?"

I could take one now, and one later. I could always come back.

And so I did, and do dream. I think too much. I am sure of this. It is madness for a young man to be so into the things of even younger years. Are we not supposed to be in the present so firmly, so concerned with this crucial present? Maybe it is the present that is the lost cause, maybe it is the past that is crucial. I do go back as if I were thinking on grand old times, and they were grand, and they were somewhat old, for me anyway, and I knew I had lived eighty years in less than twenty.

The Dead Call You By Name

I was sitting on the wall that overlooked the woods and the river, trying to push out the dark memories of last night. In shadow at the end of the street bathed in orange light, with the low sound of the river in the background, came the voice.

"Hey, Writer."

I shook my head. Ghosts. That is all it was, ghosts stuck in my head. It was windy, like the day he left. The incident had been explained away. I watched as my friend was destroyed before me. I did nothing. But he was gone. There is no rational reason for what I thought I saw. It was a trick of the light, I was tired. All the explanations went through my mind. None of them fit. I had seen him, he had been very real. His voice was the same, his clothing was the same as last I saw him. I couldn't explain it. I walked for a while by the river. I was watching the water, when I felt the presence. I looked up

29

and saw a black coated figure down the river. He was holding a long stick with one end in the stream, the water flowing around it.

"Do you remember what you told me, Writer?"

I sat on a rock. He, still holding the stick in the river, walked slowly towards me, jauntily stepping over rocks.

"You said that you would not write, that you had quit." He paused, smiling. "But of course you hadn't. Maybe you had, and all you needed was a little trauma, a little loss, to push you back into action. Maybe to really be a writer, you needed just a little bit more of the darkness. The sad, grey voice in your head that pulls you down. You have felt it often. It is there, on the edge of your consciousness, waiting for you. And just as soon as you let it, it will take you."

I opened my eyes. The grass behind my head was wet, my mind drunk and tired. Darkness lay over the forest.

I came back the next day. I had to get it over with. Either it ended here, or I would be haunted the rest of my life.

It was dawn, it was quite, and a book set nearby on a rock.

"A little early to be up isn't Writer?"

He appeared, as always, down the river some, sitting on a boulder, or walking by the river.

"Still wearing that jacket, I see."

"Why do you keep coming back? There is nothing good for you here."

"Nothing good. So there is something bad for me here?"

"Things you don't want to realize, things you left behind for a reason."

I saw my chance to hit at the problem.

"I had nothing to do with what happened to you."

He blames me. I don't know why, but he does.

"You haven't answered my question." He laughed a little as he said this, smiling. He is happier now it seems.

"Why do I keep coming back? Because you keep calling my back, because you keep being here."

"No, that won't do. You make the decision to come back. You feel guilty. You think that it was your fault. You want me to release you from your angst."

I didn't say anything. A bird flew between us.
"You think that you could have stopped me, that there was something you could have done."
"I had no idea what you planned, I never saw it coming."
"Don't give me that. You flipping knew that I was crazy, that I would do what I had to."
"I didn't know you as well as you think I did. I am just a kid, just a little nothing. I have nothing to do with that lot, with any of that stuff."
"You think you could have stopped them. They would have gotten me no matter what you did. I was already gone when I took my first breath."
"You don't know that."
"You can't know anything for sure Tim, Tim. Except that you will die someday. I made a choice. I decided to join that lot. Maybe because I was an idiot, maybe because I wanted to do something I thought was right. Probably both. We all look plenty stupid in hindsight."
"Stop being so poetic. Why didn't you tell me first? Why would you just leave, just get in a car with someone you barely knew? You chose to be an idiot."
"Ouch, that cuts to the heart Tim, Tim. "

"Stop calling me that. You lost our friendship when you chose them over me, when you chose to die."

"You think I chose to die? That would be stupid, just like me. I didn't choose death over you, Tim. I chose to avenge my father. He made a choice to stand up for what he thought was right. I had to do the same. They put him to his knees and shot him in the head. Let the Catholics go. Do you know how that feels? To know your father was killed because of who he was, and that there was nothing you could have done to stop it? Do you know what it is like to feel that powerless?"

"We are all powerless. We have little choice in any part of our lives. You spent your choice. Now I have to make mine."

"What will you do, Writer?"

"I have realized something that will let me walk out of these woods and not step back in them. You don't blame me for the choice you made, I blame you for the effect it had on me. You have robbed me of my peace of mind. I will have to fight to get it back. Ha, I guess we all fight for what we want at one point or another. But getting peace won't cost me a bloody, brutal

death. My parents won't have to read about how
I was killed in the last riot."
I began walking away, and I heard his final
words.
"Don't be so sure. Everything has a price."

Trees As Prison Guards

I had been stuck in the village for years. I had
grown there, eaten, slept and breathed there, like
a prisoner waiting for his chance, building up
strength. I developed my strength through books,
and by writing what, in captivating my soul,
freed my mind. When this is your perception,
everything is your captor, and quickly turned to
tormentors. Every tree, every building, and every
little village person held me down; everyone of
them killed me. I would escape into reading at
the library. It was small and ran campaigns with
the slogan, 'save our library.' I didn't want to save
anyone; I couldn't even save myself from myself.
For some people the best thing to do is get them
away from themselves. Their minds are chaos,
they die daily. They are taken up a hill of
crucifixion even when they sit in a library, they
breath their last breath even when it is one of
many. It is in context that a thing becomes the
greatest of hells or the sweetest of heavens. We
kill ourselves by seeing ourselves as being killed.
I could see only one way out of this tiny

shrinking world of small libraries and little
grocery stores, and little village people, I had to
be a best-selling author, a scholar of the highest
order. I needed to dwarf Aristotle, to minimize
the achievements of Dickens, and to make
Hemingway look like a wanna-be. These things
never took place, and they shouldn't. I was
stupid, I knew everything and nothing. The
intellectual children know much, and in this
paralyzing obsessive knowing, they know their
deep and confused view of life only. We must get
older, and we must live. This time will end, this
time of ourselves, this time of being captivated by
our own thoughts, of at once knowing nothing,
being a traitor to oneself, hating the earth we
walk on, and then making reparations,
understanding everything, grasping the meaning
completely, and getting back on our own side. I
die daily. I betray myself daily. I rethink my
whole life daily. I do not wish I were dead, only
that I were more simple. The simple I envy, for
they can do without thought. They can act
without being jolted by the agonizingly ceaseless
self. The hyper-active mind. You are confused
because you will not do, also because you lie to

yourself and these lies create a blockade. You look for absolutes, when there are only moments, you look for complete meaning when there is only feeling, when thought is temporal and the meaning a ghost. You live the best way to derive meaning but not the best way to derive enjoyment. Enjoyment is passion, and without passion we are without meaning to live. When enjoyment is meaningful I believe it is increased, just as sex with someone you love is not 'meaningless sex' and is therefore 'purposeful' and therefore better. Many things are an end unto themselves. Life, we decide, must be about more than living, it must be a quest, a search for the higher purpose. Maybe the purpose is not higher, maybe there is no purpose but to live and die, and to do so honorably. Enjoy what you have weather it be a fluke or God. This is practical and I believe, through the procurement of wisdom and common sense, possible. But this is not enough for me, no it is not enough for most. Most ignore it, most ignore the bird in the tree, his purpose and what he wishes to do, but for me, the trees are still my captors.

When It's Time To Leave The Castle

My mind goes back, and I am once again forced into the darkness of the courtyard. Once again forced to the castle I left, to the things I have tried to forget.

A shudder creeps over me as I walk into the barren courtyard, seemingly coming from the cold stone walls. I look back at the tower, standing tall, looming over the dark courtyard. I shuffle over the grass until I hear the crunching of gravel and see an unmoving knight on his rigid horse. There is a thought that keeps coming back to me, a conversation. I hear the crack of metal, then the grinding slide of steel on steel as the gate falls downward. At the very onset, I feel the cold, tightening rush through my body from my head to my legs. I yell as if asking for help and with a sluggish hyper push, fall backwards onto my back. I see the gate for a moment in mid-air, then my head feels warm.

I am cold when I awake. I don't move for a

moment, afraid to look and see my legs speared by the thick, rusty spikes of the gate. I breath in and look down. My feet has cleared the holes where the gate now rests by less than an inch. When I breath out, though, I realize I haven't been completely lucky. My head whirls and I now feel that the bottom of my skull rests on something hard. I know already what I have landed on. The rock has a blunt point and rests perfectly on the back of my head. I know this without even looking. I find I am able to move. 'That's a good sign. I think'. I roll to my knees. Looking up to the tower, I take in a sharp, painful breath. I saw a glint of something in the window of the tower. Standing, I walk towards the tower. The big wooden door swings open easily. Music fills the room. It has an ouara to it, like it is made of light. I begin climbing the twisting staircase up to the tower. My vision is blurred, and I feel my way up the stairs, holding myself steady on the cold rock.

An old man sits at the chess set.
"What's your name?"
I don't answer.

"Come now, what's your name?"

"Who are you. How did you get in here. You're not allowed to be here."

"I am not allowed to be here. You are telling me what I am not allowed to do?

"Yes."

He asks like it is funny.

"How did you get in here". A question I really couldn't answer.

"You know, I don't know my name. I have forgotten myself. Ever since I started to work at this castle I have slowly lost myself."

Oh, so he is an employee. But why is he still here? I lock up. I don't remember ever seeing him. Maybe he is related to the girl in the gift shop, doing some part time work. What does he mean by 'lost himself' though?

"Are you an employee here?"

"I work here. Ha, I live here nearly. My soul is stuck here."

"So you're a ghost then," I say, partly joking.

"No. I used to be a writer. Then I got sick of it all, moved down here and started work at this castle.

"I am a writer as well." I said. "Or, I was".

"It's funny that you should change it."

"Change what?"

"You said 'am' than changed it to 'was'. Are you ashamed of what you are, sorry, 'were'."

"No. I just didn't feel it anymore."

"Feel what?"

I think for a moment. 'The feeling I got when I wanted to write. I lost the soul of writing, the feeling I got deep within me from creating."

"You see yourself as a creator than?"

"Yes. And an artist."

"Oh, yes. That was always a concern. I am an artist. Not just a creator, but a creator of something useful. Of something important. That is what it is all about anyway, right? Being important."

"I guess."

"Did it lose its importance."

"What?"

"Writing."

"No. Writing is still important. It captures something of humanity that no other form can."

"The unguarded essence of thought?"

"Yes. Exactly. That is how I once put it."

"So, what are you now?"

" What am I now. What do you mean?"
"What are you? You know what the question means."
Strangely, I do know. It has been on my mind for a long time.
"I," He turns his head slightly in my direction, "I am nothing."

In The Forest

Timothy saw the trees more than the sun shining through them. Soon it would be dark, and they would be in the woods. The boy beside Timothy was older, with flat, long hair, and tight blue jeans. He always wore a jacket and his body seemed to be built in a slouching position. A voice came from up front, "Some of the kids want a picture." It was his mother. The car stopped and after a few skinny kids hopped out to pose in front of the forest entrance pictures with a small digital camera and then lope back, smiling and pointing out how strangely they smiled, the van began moving again. There were three crosses positioned in a triangle at the top of the stone arch entrance. Timothy thought of the church with a spiral top that he had passed once when it was raining, and the black-coated mass of bodies moving out of the building, with black umbrellas over their heads. The mountain adjacent the forest was a distant thing, a towering thing. He didn't understand it; sometimes he thought of people climbing the mountain and that someday he would climb it as well, but it was all very vague in his mind, like all things people think they will do, but don't.

As usual, Timothy was ahead of them all. They moved behind him in thick black clothing. A few of the younger ones wore layers that soaked through within a few minutes of real rainfall. He walked down the first steep path quickly, his feet slapping down with each step as gravity pushed him down. He thought of climbing a tree to his right but let it pass; out of the corner of his eye, the mountain dissolved. The trail curved and he plodded down the steepening walk into the forest. At the end of the first path, covered in moss like the entrance to a water cave, was a tunnel a few feet in diameter. The voices behind him faded and he heard the tunnel's echo, and, over a rock wall, down a few feet, the stream's reverent silence. Walking beside the river, listening to the water, he remembered seeing someone baptized. What came to him was the unfocused design of a memory. There was a square metal tub, behind that a white wall. People stood around the tub, watching something. Timothy could't quite see their faces, only certain features like red hair, or he imagined their features as wrinkled or heavy, but couldn't make it out directly. A man with large, careful hands stood over the tub, directing with his movement. A man sat in the tub wearing a blue robe, his eyes were shut, the palms of his hands supported him on the seat which rose out of the plastic lining of the tank. The man with big hands took hold of the man's head, and began speaking. He bellowed something out, then stopped. He looked down and everyone around the tank let out yells in different degrees, as sounds came from deep within their chests as if experiencing pleasure. People spoke very mechanically and continued to stare ahead either at the man in the tank or the white wall. The speaker began again and after a few more stops and starts, his voice rising and falling with emphasis on each crescendo and decent, he lowed his voice and spoke in a conclusion. Then the man's head was pushed back under the water.

The path turned to gravel. Up ahead light shown where the trees thinned then disappeared all together as the trail met the river on a bank of rocks. The light was so bright as to make the gravel look like pure light. Timothy approached and looked into the woods. Each tree was spaced a few feet from each other. The floor of the forest lay covered in what looked like short brown hay, and under that, patches of moss, made more green by the grey trees, mystical-looking with limbs hanging low to the ground. He remembered that C.S. Lewis was inspired by these woods to write Narnia. Timothy had seen the movie, but had not read the books. Timothy was disappointed. There were no lions in these woods, no witches, no groups of English kids turned into kings and queens, no talking animals. Timothy only heard silence, only saw the trees, the brown hay, the narrow bars of light streaming through the less dense foliage. He turned and walked slowly to the rocky bank. Water flowed between the rocks. He looked through the trees. The sky had grayed, and through the murky light he saw, looking like two large ants, two figures, like large ants, climbing the mountain. He heard voices down the path, distant, but coming towards him.

One Immortal Thing

I walked by the dark river. It flowed up to the
dam. It would flow more fiercely with rain.
Things seemed very empty to me. Not the natural
things, not the wind, or the water, or the trees.
They were the same. But what I wrote, what I
use to write, it did not make sense anymore. I felt
everything, and nothing. I paid close attention to
the wind and its tone, but the words of all those
around me fell silent, like voices muffled. Even
when I tried to focus, I felt far away from them.
As if on a boat, where the harder I rowed, the
further I moved out to sea. Well, it was all
nonsense. It was all nothing. And it was my own
fault. I put myself through hell. I made my life a
tiny pinhole. At night, I would watch the lake,
and in the quite it felt as if my soul were dying. I
was a writer before I was anything else. But
being a writer had made me nothing but that. I
had come to a point with myself where I was the
only one I knew. I thought, and kept on thinking,
and I kept on doing so in circles. And now I
didn't know what else to do. For the fact that I

could not live because of my writing made my living an impossibility. Writing flows from life, and I only wrote about not writing, or things being stopped up, or not working. This is a true point: I have never worked. A few parts of me seem different, connected to something. For a while I thought I had great potential, then I realized I struggled more with living then understanding anything else. And I did not want to be the struggling writer or artist. I hated it. Life was better. We are a breed that becomes, through the trait of self-centeredness and ego, fixated on one part of the mind, trying to hone it to rise above. Then at some point we realize we are only gaining and losing inches, and that those who rise far above do so without trying, like they have stopped struggling and decided to flow with the stream instead of against it. They are great because of their ability to live. It gives to their ability to write. To live is the point, to write derives the meaning. We give meaning in our writing; we use our life, but we only do one part of the operation, and soon we have nothing to give meaning to, nothing to express but old themes. I understood it all clearly, but I could do nothing. It became worse as I grew older. I am still young, but it doesn't matter.

The truth is, we don't rise or fall; things just happen, and we react. One thing set everything going. That would be God or the Big Bang. Either life originated from a father figure who loves us and lives in the clouds, or it is the result of an incident which we call the 'big bang', a name that sounds like a child describing what happened when he knocked over a lamp. We don't know anything. The sooner we except that the easier life becomes. A caveman couldn't grasp the concept of an airplane, and even he would get it more than we understand the reality of life. We are emotional animals, and anything we know is affected by the fact that we can't see correctly. It is the reason why one person can look at the setting of the sun and see the day ending and another sees the night beginning.

The cabin at night was too quite. The concerns which he could not quell came to him, and as he closed his eyes he felt two ideas grow closer. He felt terrible as they drew closer, and as they touched, his eyes shot open and he expected to see satan in the darkness. Outside it was cold and clear and the moon put out a blue tint. The wind felt like God, and the clear water seemed motherly, protecting. He put his bare feet on the grainy rock and waited for the white breath morning. He dreamed. Quite streets, quite floating figures. He walked and kept turning corners. He kept turning to find nothing. Then, after some time, he came upon a dock. It led to a dull white boat. In it was a figure. He started down the dock with urgency. The water surged and the boat began moving further out. As he reached the end of the dock, the boat was out of his reach. The sun rose by the mountains in the distance and blinded him. He could just make out the blurry figure through his fingers, staring straight ahead into the blinding sun.

He woke to the sound of birds, and the sloshing of water, and the sun in his eyes. "Keep your head clear." He said it like the mantra it had become. "Don't kill yourself for nothing." The day was empty, he needed something to do. It was dangerous for him to have nothing. Silence was painful, worse than wrong thoughts. Silence was death. The boat lay in the inlet to his right. The cabin was warm behind him. His feet and hands were numb. He went inside to eat.

You try to fix a boat, and the whole world's against you. It had always been like that; everything is always harder than it should be. Things break too easily. There is no point in using anything, it all breaks so quickly. I was standing in the cabin, in the kitchen. This is usually my favorite time, with the sun coming in lightly through the windows; the wall towards the lake has only small windows at the top, as it would be too hot in the summer for larger ones. But the small porch has windows looking out onto it, and I would put a chair out there and drink coffee and read. I wouldn't stay when it rained because the roof over the porch was too short and even if the wind was light the rain came in easily. Thinking about the boat made me too upset to stay inside. It was always this way: I had something I wanted to do, and just couldn't.

God himself would come down to stop me from getting to it. Not this time. I grabbed my tool set. They had been advised to wait. For what reason? I don't know. But I did know that I could get the boat patched up enough to fish safely in the shallow. The clouds were dark. I set down my coffee and grabbed some toast to eat as I walked to the boat on the side of the little inlet by the shore. The ultra clear water showed the circle stones of the bed, the kind of stones you could put on a mantel or your desk. The boat was flipped over to expose its underside and there was a hole the size of a fist. I had never repaired a boat, but I could figure it out as I went. That tended to be the best way to do things. If you thought too much, you never got started. A skill is to use, not think about. Some people learn the piano and never do it again until they're forty, and then they can only remember chopsticks. The rain started up as I walked towards the garage to get the patch material, as if heaven really were against me, throwing light jabs to test my resolution. The garage was closed and I thought that it may be locked, but the smaller door was open.

I stood at the door. It was a large garage, not big enough to get lost in but big enough to be confused. On the other side of some bikes, behind a tool set, on a shelf, I found what I needed in a small metal box. I looked around at the packed garage. It seemed hopeless; there were so many useless things. Boats broke, and were left broken. People die, dreams die; we work towards something our whole lives, just trying to make one masterpiece, one immortal thing, and we are dashed against the rocks just like that boat. But then, there is no one to patch us up.

I came out and saw the sun shining over the lake. The rain had stopped. The boat lay wet and broken. It made me think of a painting, one expressing some idea. The sun shinning over the broken hull, the lake clear and beautiful in the background. Well, anyway, that's stupid. I went over and began to fix the boat. After an hour I took a break and ate lunch. I looked at the boat through the window, thinking about it. Something had come to mind. In a little dusty

box under the coffee table is where I keep my
manuscripts, written on a portable, old fashioned
typewriter, with notes scribbled on them. I took
out a paper and went to sit by the lake. It began:

"I lost my comrade. He had fallen in the mental
battle, no, the mental war, of thoughts, strong,
moving, animating the face and hands to speak
lies. Lying to ourselves and to others constantly;
too confused, too self-diluted to see past our
hands on which we write that which is important:
be a doctor, be a priest, be a writer. But why?
We go too far and stop at death, we go too far
and stop at the beginning of life. We are trapped
here, in the stage that is the middle. And isn't it
ironic that we don't see the comparison right
away. It's like a play. Religion, science, any idea,
are just subjects discussed to make it interesting,
the drama between the cast is just to make it
interesting. Loving and leaving, and wanting, and
being hopeful, its all just to have something to do,
all for the sake of the drama.
I had enough of myself."

It was untitled. I smiled. A cold, bracing wind

picked up. I felt the grass under me, and the solid rock at my feet, and the clearness of the water. From that mental abstractness, I had grown, I had moved on. I had gotten better at living. From the self-absorbed intellectual banter of my childhood, I had become a man, and struggled with real things, like loss and regret, and crippling confusion. I had moved on from the analysis paralysis of my past and on to feel the pain of a dream dying, and felt great about it. Even when life goes from one pain to another, more mature pain, it is still progression. It is not useless suffering, which would be actual suffering, rather than the pain that makes us greater, which, though it hurts, brings promise of self growth. I knew my pain was not senseless, and this brought me peace. I could see where I had gotten better from my old pain, and how this pain was making me into something even greater. If in our minds we think the pain does not help, we destroy ourselves, our chances of making it through. But if we change our perception, and see each moment of pain as elevating us to greatness, that it moves us beyond the mundane little concerns of the rest of the human race, then we could become our full selves. That is what I have wanted all along anyway, to be far from small concerns, to really be great, not just in appearance. I wanted greatness to be intrinsic, for it to be a science that I had mastered. I didn't want a spotlight, I wanted to die nobly, giving myself for a greater cause, so that at my death I would think, 'you have done it. You are truly the best you could have been. And I would feel that those I love were proud that I had done what only I could do. I had succeeded at being human, and at being really good at it.'

I stood slowly and went to the boat. I started working right away, happy to feel the tools in my hand.

I could fix this. It is all fixable. We just keep learning. I will learn this. The manuscript floated in the water where I left it, soaking through, sinking into the water. I could see it go for a while. I glanced over once to see it fading, but didn't look again.

The Gilford Collection

Little Else

''I would like to have one or two, possibly three great moments in my life.''
 The husband stood close to his wife. They were on a little patio. Tea was on inside. ''Moments in which I exceed wisdom. I become the values I hold dear. Few live up to their values, so I believe that this will be enough. Just a few times.''
The wife thought very little about what the husband said. It wasn't that she didn't love him, but he talked about this often. It meant nothing, or very little at most. What can a man say that is different from anyone else? We cannot say anything new, she accepted this. But her husband lived somewhere else. She wished she could go where he went. But she would not understand it.
''We must take a stand, put ourselves out there,'' he went on to say. ''There is little

else we can do but take a stand." The sun
came down slowly and he suddenly became
very tense, as if waiting for a battle to
begin. "We have nothing else. We have
very little else."

He felt sad, and he knew, now , that all
those books on his nightstand and the
papers at his desk meant nothing, he had
just now killed them. 'I guess they were to
go sometime,' He thought. Even now the
walk down to breakfast had become cold.
The hardwood floor felt cold, the sun
through the window seemed dull. Life was
a quietly dying animal, and he was just
talking to put it out of its misery.

The Wind Around Trains

The stream took everything away. If something were to land in it, it would be taken away to somewhere else. Timothy thought about pushing off on the small raft that had been built by a few local kids from wood littering the forest floor, to flow smoothly down the river, under the bridge, to somewhere else. And as the scenery around him changed, he would be so deliriously happy, as if things were becoming more alive, more mystical. He would think happily, 'I wonder where I am headed? I wonder how far am I from Gilford? What waits for me ahead?"
He thought of his small, dark room at home. The fear he felt when the door shut. Would it be his mother's hand or his father's shoe and the cold concrete of their doorstep. 'No,' he thought, ' I can't. They will find me.

So he started back on his walk home. 'Besides, things weren't that bad. They could be much worse.' Things were not the worst that they could be. He would get along okay.

'Just stay quite, and keep your head down,' he thought.

So what if things weren't perfect. They weren't perfect anywhere. He felt somewhat comforted, a reprieve from worry. But as he approached his home, he felt the same, old hallow fear. It was empty now, like the fear had become a natural reaction to the sight of his home. The word didn't seem to fit this place. The idea did not fit his reality.

He decided that, if he were good, they would see, they would see this time. He would be so nice, so happy and loving, that they would have to respond in kind; the joy would catch. He felt happy with this idea, with this new plan. He had tried other plans before. But this was simple, and it made sense that it would work. Love begets love.

He entered the house slowly, trying to look natural. He said loudly, "is anyone here"?

No answer. The house was cold and silent, as if a bomb had went off nearby and everyone had evacuated. He went to his room, did his homework, and played with his toys, of which he had three. One was an old robot, most likely based off an eighties cartoon, another was a small man wearing a belt with two grenades attached, and the last was a little train, blue, the paint chipped and scratched. He pushed the train around, the man with the grenades sitting on top, and placed the robot in front as if it were blocking the tracks.

"Get out of the way," he yelled "You'll be run over," he giggled. Then he had a thought, he could place his train with the man and the robot in front of the door. That would be a great way to start his new initiative to make them love him. They would think it funny. He was already laughing to himself, imagining when they came in and saw this weird, orchestrated train wreck. When he heard the car, he ran to the front door and placed the train just to the side of it. The next few moments were silent and tense. He peered from behind the wall, expectantly waiting for the door to swing open and his father or mother to see the train. Timothy was more than pleased with the setup. It would be a nice start to the new life he planned. The car door opened. Silence.

The door shut. Footsteps. Someone jingled the keys, trying to get them into the lock, like they couldn't stop their hand from shaking. Timothy began to worry that it was stranger, a burglar who had found the spare key. He hid shrank behind the wall, peering at the door that could possibly reveal the face and body of an intruder. The key finally made contact. The handle began to turn. The door creaked opened some, as if lightly pushed, then, in one fast motion, swung open, loudly crashing into the wall. His father stood in the doorway, holding a dark colored bottle. His posture reminded Timothy of a zombie. He was bent over, holding the bottle with three fingers, his face empty, white, and dead, as if someone had sucked the human out of him. For a moment Timothy thought he wouldn't notice the train. Then he looked down and moved forward, staggering. He even moved like a zombie, Timothy thought. Timothy was in such near ecstasy when his father smiled slightly, that he forgot about the near empty bottle, and what that bottle did to him, who it made him when he held it. It was almost mystical to Timothy, like the bottle was a sacred artifact that changed those

who held it. He had found one in a bush outside
the house one day, (probably from his father
when he would drink out there before coming
in.) He had tentatively held it in his hands, and
waited to feel differently. He hadn't, and still
could't explain why his father seemed affected by
it and he didn't. Did the stuff inside change who
you were? Maybe it was a sacred liquid instead.
If so, it didn't do much for his father's
appearance. He looked worse every time he came
back from wherever he got the bottles. And he
now looked worse than Timothy had ever seen
him, as if he really were the dead walking. When
his father's face turned from the slight smile into
an angry scowl, it was almost nightmarish. His
countenance seemed to transform into something
evil, as if something deep inside had shifted as
well, as if he had become the look on his face.
Timothy was young, but he knew quickly that
this was not his father, this was someone else,
someone the bottle made, the liquid, or the bottle
itself, or both. This was someone who belonged
to the bottle. He was no longer Heckle and
Hyde, he was just Hyde, just the demon, made
into something Timothy didn't understand.

Timothy wished for the other man, who was now just a ghostly shadow of what he used to be, but was still better than this hellish figure. Timothy was so afraid that he sank to his knees, already crying, as the demon moved toward him, eyes fiery, predator-like, crushing his little train. He both felt and didn't feel the fingers strongly gripped around his ear, yanking him backwards.

The beating lasted for what seemed like hours, until the father stood above him, out of breath, the belt loosely hanging in his hand. Timothy curled into the fetal position, covering his head and face. He was usually able to protect his face from most of it. He had gotten good at getting out of the beating with as little hurt as possible, but this time was different. He had been kicked and thrown against the wall, and when he reached down to hold his aching body, the belt had come strong and hard against his face. He felt a sharp sting, and then the blood from his nose and the throbbing.
The demon had began to lose steam, he was distracted by something outside the window. Timothy limped off, holding his nose, wishing

with all his heart that the demon wouldn't turn around, and beat him even harder as if in response to movement. The door had been open the whole time, so he was able to slip out silently. He went to his room and found a shirt to dab the blood from his face. He sat on his bed, not thinking. The pain wiped out any thought. The pain had always made him silent. This pain was mostly silent, except for one thought. He would love to be on that train, with the wind blowing over him, in his eyes and hair. Going off to nowhere. Off into the clouds. He looked out the window, towards the road he had come up.

He grabbed some clothes, the first few things he saw, then slowly, quietly, walked down the hall. When he came to his parents door, he froze. He thought that his father would have passed out by now, but he heard a sound. His father said something, he slurred it out. Timothy didn't move a muscle. He could see himself floating down the river, watching the trees on the banks, lying down and closing his eyes, breathing in the wind. He stayed completely still. When he heard his father suck in air sharply and snore out some incoherent babble, he felt more relief than he had ever felt. It flooded his mind and body, like a cool, refreshing shower. He began walking towards the front door then turned to look back at the beast that had transformed back into his father, his silent then quietly rambling father, stretched out over the bed, the blankets torn in all directions. Timothy's blood was splattered on the floor nearby. He walked back to his father, pushed his tussled hair back, and kissed his forehead. He hugged him and cried bitterly. He would never be what he wanted, what for a small moment he had been. When things had gotten harder, when they had less money, when jobs became scarce, and his lack of expertise had become too much of an obstacle to deal with sober, he had started on the journey to this creature that lay in front of him. He loved the father through the demon that had stolen him. He didn't want to let go, but he did.

He left without looking back. He knew if he did he would not be able to leave. He would start to forget about the pain as it lessened, and things would go on as they were. He felt where he knew the red mark was on his face, the mark of the demon. And he envisioned what it would be like, free on that stream, laying back, watching the wind blow the trees. He walked towards the door, stopping to pick up the small man and put it in his pocket, and take the front piece of the train.

He had looked back the whole walk to the stream, feeling more and more at ease as he gained distance from his home. He moved as quickly as he could, trying not to draw attention, keeping his head low to hide his face. He reached the wall by the road overlooking the small forest in the middle of the village and the river that rain through it. He looked down; the river was there, waiting for him. As he started walking to the gate of the forest, he saw a car out of the corner of his eye that he thought was his mother's. Fear struck him, then faded quickly. It wasn't his mother. But he would not be afraid, even if it were, not anymore. He was already gone. He had already made the choice. And very soon he was walking down the path to the bank of the river

At the bank, the little raft was sitting half on land and half in the water, still tied to a stump. He easily unloosened the rope, then pushed the raft onto the water with little effort. It floated pretty well. He held it with his hand, stepped on, and went to his knees. The raft slowly moved forward, pushed by the current. He started moving more quickly as he neared the narrow area under the bridge. For a while he was clipping along, clearing distance quickly. He was out of sight of the gate and the wall, the bridge growing smaller, then disappearing behind a bend. He was now on the river, truly headed to nowhere. He felt safer and happier the more distance he gained. And then, there was a point, where it all left his mind, and he was watching the trees, laying back on the raft that bobbed lightly, smoothly passing the trees, and flowing down the river. He pulled out the little man and the piece of the train and set them at the front of the raft, positioning the little piece that had been on the front of the train in front of the man, and the little man sitting, with his hand raised, as if saying "Off to nowhere".

The Gilford Collection

The Doctor And The Patient

"I had the dream again, this time worst than the last."
"Really? What was it about?"
Her long, pristine face was turned towards the window. Her eyes rested in the direction of the monument and the lions that were positioned around it. As a little girl she had watched the lions as she went through town with her parents. They made her feel safe, like guardians. Now they represented the naiveness of her youth.
'There are no guardians.' She thought.
"We are left to ourselves."
"What do you mean?" The doctor set back in his chair and made an inquisitive face.
"Nothing."
She thought for a moment. 'Why not really talk to him. It doesn't matter.'
"I have never been able to believe in anything," she said.
"Like what? God?"
" As a child my father was very religious. He is no longer religious. My mother died and God

died with her."
"He couldn't believe in God because his wife
died?"
"He chose to punish God, as if his wife were the
only one that would be spared from this natural
occurrence.
In anything, can we assume to know? We ask
about those tortured and killed as children, and
suffering in other countries; We ask about the
Nazis and what the people subjected under them
went through, the suffering in the concentration
camps. What are these things really? Pain.
Humiliation. Anguish. It is the body and mind
having things inflicted upon them. If your wife
were raped, say, and you were nearby and could
have done something, or you were powerless to
do something, this is where you would scream at
God: 'Help me. Save me. Give me the power to
overcome this.' And as many times before, God
would not answer.
So, does God exist and is evil, or is he a concept
we have created in order to feel good, to feel
comfortable. That is why my father believed in
him, because it was comfortable. C.S. Lewis said
that if you come to religion looking for comfort

you will find soft-soap, niceties, nothing of value.
If you live by a fire only for the comfort of the
fire, never understanding the fundamentals of
your comfort, someday that fire may go out as
you did not know how to maintain it or build a
new one. If you had come to the concept of fire
with the right concern, you would have learned
to build one. Your sights would have been set on
the deeper matters of understanding rather than
the shallow matters of feeling. If you reside in the
shallow, you get beat by the tide, by your's and
other's whims and fancies. That's all well and
good, but there does seem to be a lot of things
wrong with the basic concept of God and how he
works. Why would he punish people for their
mistakes? Children who have been taught by
their parents excel because of what they know;
parents who punish children instill negative
energy within their minds and teach them
nothing other than that they will occasionally feel
pain. They learn to fear, not to excel. God, in this
context, seems to be an ill-equipped parent. Even
birds know to teach off-spring by example. Do
this to fly. The children learn to fly in short order.
If the mother were to beat them, it would do little

to help them fly. In fact it would associate a
negative feeling of trying to fly with pain and
failure.

Why send someone to hell? It is pointless. We
have little hand in making ourselves the way we
are. We have minds to learn. Pain is a guard to
keep us safe. In this sense, pain and suffering
excel us only in our knowledge of what will hurt
us. We do not always listen. We experience pain
and, out of self-interest, decide to stay away from
that thing. But for pain to continue forever,
teaches us nothing. It is pain for the sake of pain.
Instruct us, we do not hear. Hurt us, we listen.
We move forward. But hurting us forever when
we have little ability to understand that which we
should not do is pointless. If Hitler experienced
all of the pain he had inflicted; two times that
pain, three times that pain, would that not be
enough? He was only one man, subject to the
way he was made and the environment he lived
in. Why not teach him the wrongness of his ways
before he lived out his fate and be done with it. It
is the most inefficient system ever invented, the
punishment philosophy of the Bible, as it offers
no way to be better after the punishment, only

eternal damnation for something we had very little choice in.

I should point out that this is not how things are; these are only ideas and concepts. I am one human subject to bias speaking to other humans subject to bias. I am very limited in my understanding of the things we can know, and there are many things I cannot know due to the nature of my being. I can simply ask questions and discuss these matters for the sake of it."

The doctor's head bobbled for the duration of the speech.

"There are many problems on the other side as well, my dear. If we come from the depths of evolution, and evolution posits that our prime motivator is to exist, than why are we always doing things that are opposite of that directive? Killing ourselves and others, not taking proper care of ourselves. Consciousness itself makes no sense. Consciousness gets in the way of survival and is rather pointless. We are here to exist? That is it? There is no reason we should be able to conceptualize God and dying. Without God we fear death, and yet we cannot believe because

he makes no sense to us. Consciousness should
not exist without God. Does God exist without
consciousness? To us, no. But I think this is the
wrong way to look at it. Are we meant to
understand? We understand nothing: not why he
made us, not what heaven is like if it exists, not
what God is like or what God really is; we
understand nothing. We can learn to live better
but we have no understanding of anything else.
We are meant to live, as well as we can.
I see it like an endless cave. We stand in one part
of it, our knowledge lights the immediate area,
but the cave is endless. We see others with their
lights all over and we think we know a lot, but
the cave is endless. No matter the wisdom we
come upon, we will never reach the full size of
the cave. We like to say the impossible is possible
because it is good rhetoric. "We can do it" is filled
with hope. So we choose the emotion over the
reality, as usual. This allows the emotion to drive
us. We fear the revelation of the truth because it
may take away our hope, but if we were to search
for the truth instead, we would have no fear."
This is all just a part of it: the conspiracy of life.
The secret to living is realizing that it is its own

reason. What else can we do? If we vanquish evil but cannot define it, if we find hope but do not keep it, if we understand just to be baffled, what is the reason we vanquish, the reason we find, the reason we seek to understand? For the sake of it? Because there is nothing else to do?

She left, and the silence remaining during the parting said all that could be said. Back to the conspiracy, then.
I looked out my office window. The rain blanketed the grayness and the iron lions stood like guardians over nothing.

Part Two

''I had been writing a memoir at the
time. I had written for three months,
while also working on the boat tours
down the Liffey. 'And there's so and
so avenue, and there's another
monument named after someone none
of you know.' Some of them had
heard of Parnell, but most could only
envision the Irish as a drunken
comrade-in-arms type people. They
could be literary, they were tuff, they
had a sense of humor, they were
drunk, and they fought a lot among
themselves. This is what the tourist
wearing a hat that says 'Kiss Me I'm
Irish' knows. He finds joy in thinking

he is connected to something older
them himself, more important, more
mystic and historical. It is the fact that
people cannot find anything they
deem important within themselves
that they must feel connected to
something bigger, something
important. And we all of course love
solidarity, the feeling that we are
together with others, which is
different from being physically
together with others. We fear
isolation, so we force the feeling of
solidarity with people we don't know,
people with whom we may have
nothing in common. Because, after all,
my great, great, great, grandfather
was born on the same plot of land as
you. We are real blood brothers."

Celebrate Murder

The pub, where fat men threw up outside, was my sanctuary. It was where I escaped the mix of fleshy, somehow sweaty in sixty degree weather bodies. I was sitting at the corner table where I could monitor who came in. I had at least an hour before the whole parade emptied out of town. I imagined leaving this village, ridding myself of its bonds. In the river that flowed through, in the the little stores, in the short back alleys leading to small courtyards, in the rubble of an old store, in all of it, was the memory of death. It was all a place of memory, and the bitter aftertaste of that memory was old fights, pubs, drunkenness, hatred, ancient tradition. All these words were so real, as if they we intertwined with the fabric of the place, the essence, as if you could see them in the brick of every wall, and hear them in the water flowing beneath the bridge.

I had withdrawn myself from the festivities. I
went down to the bar. In the pub, among the
smoke and the soccer pictures on the wall, all the
lads smiling with arms over shoulders, I felt a
little better, like I could relax. My mind went
back to the grey morning. I had sat and drank my
coffee, reading the paper about the recent
bombings. We would kill each other alright, it
was a certainty. I would stay out of it, keep
withdrawing to the pub, keep getting just drunk
enough to burry my mind. I felt someday I
wouldn't have a pub for escape. I was losing the
will to run away, or the ability.

From the corner of my eye, I saw Clancy
come in. He had the walk of man who wants to
hurt someone. He looked towards me and his
face was a collage of anger, each muscle
expressing the emotion absolutely. His eyes held
a malevolent intelligence and his assured barking
to his boys at the bar held a contained hatred. He

was a ticking bomb, looking for someone to push the detonator. He drank for awhile. He had been just a boy at one time, then life opened up some, things took their course. After a few mishaps and run-ins with the police, Clancy became a stereotype. He was told what he was, and worst, he believed it. He was a trouble-maker, a good-for-nothing. If he was, he thought, might as well live up to it, at least he should be good at what society had named him. And from what I could tell, he was. He had nearly killed more than a few boys in school, fought his with father. (Knowing the father, he had a hand in starting those fights, which of course added to the downward cycle of the the son.) Like father like son. Beyond that he had been caught practically forcing himself on half a dozen different girls at one time or another. He was on a downward spiral, and he probably wouldn't stop until he ended up dead in a riot.

I felt anger gush up from within me, as if a geyser had irrupted. Keeping it in by clutching the table barely worked. The pressure was building. I stood and almost ran to the door, the eyes of the pub boys alert to a possible skirmish.

Outside in the bright sun, I kept hearing these words, sounding like an anthem:

'In the name of justice we murder, under the guise of good we commit evil, under the drive of hatred we take lives, and above all we seek to ruin, both ourselves, and the lives of all around us. We are chaos, and ignorance is our benefactor.'

It was truth summed up like a poem. I felt like screaming it out, but I knew, deep down, that no one would hear, that no one would ever listen. I knew these words were for me, these words were my salvation.

I would speak these words to no one. In the square, among the craziness, I moved to see the signs they were carrying. They were so proud of themselves, so happy about their hate. We are all fools, the lot of humanity. I wish we could let the younger ones forget our pathetic fights. We kill each others sons and celebrate it. I felt like the crowd around me was a disease. I started pushing, trying to get out of the sickness. I was jostled, pushed and shoved. Where are you going? Trying to get out? Why? You are no different. You are just like us. No, I am nothing like you. I may be from here, but I am not this place; I refuse my inheritance of hate, of old thought and old ways. We don't learn from the past or honor it. We validate ourselves by proving our superiority. We won, or we lost because they cheated. I could see the end of the crowd. I pushed through and found myself in a small alley. I watched them go, all together, like a cavern to hell. Celebrating murder, celebrating evil. I moved down the alley. I would find a way out, a way over the buildings, and then I would walk the hills, I would go where they could not find me. I would find a cave with a waterfall, and there, among the sprinkled, fresh air, I would remake my thoughts, there humanity would be no longer, I would be the only one to exist, and I would hold no parades.

The Promenade

Three children run the cross walk. I make my way past them, watching the sun still low on the horizon. I had come here and found that I was a walker. I would wake in my small hotel room, look out the window with mettle all around it, and see the beach. I would smile as I walked out of my room, across the old creaking floor, and down the turning staircase. I had no breakfast, and ran through the little square that all the buildings on this part of the promenade shared. In a way, it was a promenade to hell. I walked this beach for hours. I had walked three miles the first day, increasing that number every day. Afterwards I walk till my feet are sore. I walk because it takes me away from the things that hide in my room, in my past. They all congregate there. I forgo coming home as long as possible.

When I move, they find me. So I have to keep moving, and more than that, I have to keep walking.

I will keep increasing my miles everyday, until, maybe, I will find the end of the earth. Maybe a door will be there, and I will open it. There will be someone waiting, other people rushing around, trying to prepare things, to get things together.

"Oh, thank goodness someone found us. We have been waiting for you all to wake up. Quickly, before you must go, we have some things for you to take, and we have a few things to tell you."

And then we will walk out onto a large Greek styled patio, with vines twining down large pillars. There will be a very blue ocean and to the right will be gorgeous land, filled with forests and mountains with waterfalls. And a wise man will begin to talk while his associates move quickly into the background, holding scrolls.

"Humanity has failed greatly. I know that is what you expect to hear, and you are right. They say there is no truth, but there is. You are one of God's experiments. He put truth out there, wisdom, to see if anyone could reach it. To see, in essence, if this experiment lived up to the goals he had set out for it. He is very skilled in these matters, but some things must be played out. A few, Socrates and Abraham Lincoln among them, succeeded to some degree in the pursuit of truth. Many others, most others, have failed. You are the wild card, the unknown in the group. We will use you; you are the workaround, the loophole in the system. See, you weren't supposed to be made. It was a mistake. But it was a good one. We need you to save humanity. We have to go. Here, take this."

He will hand me a scroll.

"We will most likely not meet again. You won't fail. I have seen it."

Then they will all walk to a far wall where a

pillar will open, and the wise man and his associates will enter and it will blast off over the blue ocean. I will stand there, with the parchment in my hands, and think nothing.

There are other reasons I walk the beach. I am looking for something. I have never been able to accept my family's ideas on religion. Not because I don't believe them, but because I hate dependance. Dependence is weakness. I cannot need people. If I need someone I become vulnerable. It also means I am not strong enough, good enough to do things on my own. I not only want to be important, I want to be the most important. I am consumed with egotism and this leads to rage. I am angry about my lack of importance. I blame others for my struggles, and I despise those who have faith, who depend on something else. I see them as weak, begging dogs, hoping to be fed by their vengeful master. Of course this is all small-minded. I am just as weak and as dependent on others as they. And we are all squalling dogs if you think of it. What is hard is not to struggle, but to be okay, and in that okayness, to not be important, but to just exist with our flaws and our small thoughts.

The sun descends and all is gone. There is the faint sounds of the distant carnival on the boardwalk. It sounds like a satanic revelry, where they cooked the flesh of humans. I keep walking, trying to get away from the carnage. In the sand and the sea, the moon top right above, all the sound is gone, in a black abyss, falling through the greek patio down into the blue ocean, I was important, and then I was gone.

Two Steps From Death

It was called Spar, and when I drove up at night, the little town center lurked quite in the orange lit darkness, except for a low wind that raced through its confined alley ways. And it was completely dark, except for the dim lights of the moon hidden behind the clouds, and the orange, rough disks created by the streets lamps. It looked to me like a place forgotten. It was hard to imagine anyone going in there.

On the quite Gilford streets, I took a shallow breath, my inhale cut of by the quickening of my heart as I spun to see my attacker. There was nothing. I imagined the worst, again.

I was not brave, and I felt small standing outside the store on the dark street. I envisioned all the people, mostly older, sleeping in their town homes across the circle. It was a small community. I turned back to the Spar and unlocked the door. Inside I felt as if I were entering a crypt. Everything was a cold quite. The refrigerated section hummed silently, with the neon lights extinguished. The five aisles of dark pits. When I switched the light on, it failed to respond. I moved forward cautiously, and began probing for my forgotten item around the cash register.

When I exited onto the dark street, I felt the funniest feeling that I was not there. And then, nothing.

We Love You Trudy

It was Trudy's last day at the library and her heart felt sick. It was a deep, depressing sickness, in which the world changed color, music sounded boring, all of it, and where things began to lose their vehemence. Heavy rain swept the town's streets, causing the gutter to flow like small rivers. She watched her car through the small blurry window that showed through the little two-door entrance, and then out the windows on either side of the front door. She imagined trying to get into her car with this much rain. Her body was not so young. She had once climbed mountains in Bangladesh, rode horses in the country; she had been married. She had done so much, and like paint draining down a sink, her life had become grey. All the color was gone, only the wall, chipped and faded, remained. She stared at it and wondered what to do. She found writing on it to be unsatisfying, so she tried to imagine pictures of better times on it. It was a sad, depressing thing to do. But it was the kind of depressing that left you reminiscent. So things would end at the end of the day. She thought of going to Dingle the following day, maybe to visit the cliffs of Moore. Perhaps standing on the majestic cliffside would remind her of the largeness of life. But here, behind her desk, writing boring inventory lists and stamping books, life felt like this room. This room was all, and this room would soon be gone. In a way, her whole life was ending.

The library, tall and old in the middle of the village, where the cars passed out front, was set for demolition. They would blow it at the end of the week. Trudy, a short, heavy women with frizzy hair, wearing a thick, orange sweater, was having trouble stapling papers. In frustration, she

threw the stapler across the room. It flew past
Betty who made a quizzical expression and then
went back to stocking the kid's section, which
was a large portion of the store. The librarian
looked across the room she had worked in for
four years. Soon, all of it would be gone. She
tried to not think about it. Her heart deepened
when she did. She felt a heavy, sinking feeling,
like her lungs were being compressed by her
thoughts. Betty came over, the only other
librarian for such a small library. She smiled
stupidly, her hands coming together to rub
themselves into a tizzy, as if she were suddenly
very cold.

"It will all be over soon," she said giddily,
excited to be at the end of the day and to have
something to talk about.

"Soon they will crush this place like a
cardboard box. I found a job at the mall. You
may find something if you look. What do you say.
We could work together there maybe."

Trudy McGuire didn't answer. She had wanted to slap her assistant on more than one occasion, and this situation was no different

That night Trudy closed the door to the library. She drove slowly on the road, wet and dark, with hedge rows hugging close on one side and trees on the other. Going up the narrow stairs of her home in the suburbs, she realized, at the top, holding on to the railing tightly, that she was not going to Dingle.

The Unobserved Shelf

The smell of pot pie wafted through, past the counter, over the chairs and tables of the warm restaurant. Penny Lane played on the old radio Jeremy had brought over from his garage. He found it while setting up for a boot sale. He brought it when it didn't sell. I liked it. I liked listening to music rather than just sitting in the leather chair with the wooden back that had loopy designs in it. I enjoyed the music while eating lunch. This was contentment and I wanted more of it. I had worked for three years at this shop. And today, when I rose from my small bed, looked out the barred windows, and went to the cold, hard bathroom where the faucets leaked, I thought about the few books I rarely looked at still on a shelf. I could have sold them at the thrift shop down the street. Made a fiver. But I kept

them. Why? I wanted to be reminded of what I
had been. I was smart in high school. Good
grades. One day I had been nervous before a
presentation. My teacher took my arm and told
me I had greatness in me. I felt so assured, so
confident about myself, that I got up there and
ad-libbed most of my points. I forgot my notes
and spoke from passion. I had confidence, faith,
belief. I was excited. There was this pure
creativity in me. It was white, and this whiteness
spread to my arms and legs and rose up my neck.
That day stayed in my mind. It had been great,
but it had become my climax. I had let myself go.
I looked for the next mountaintop experience,
when life was before me. Life is one big
mountaintop experience. I was too complex, and
it ruined me.

I wanted more; I needed more. Every second I
waited, I wanted to burst out of my skin. There
was a bus stop down the street. It came to me as

a hot, then warm intuition. I smiled at it. I stood and heard the air breaks. Imagining wouldn't be enough.

On The Giants Causeway

Three figures disappeared down the steep road to the circle rocks. Today, I walked slowly, maintaining my pace, watching my footing. It was a safe walk, one of convention. I didn't look long at anything, and I didn't talk to anyone. The bus passed. Faces glared out at the ocean, and at me. In their eyes I saw nothing. Humanity raced ahead while I walked, watching my footing, making sure not to lose my balance and go barreling forward. I realized I wasn't worried about my safety, just looking like a fool. I didn't want to be a fool.

Walkways of Light

The walkways had light down them, all
through them, like angels of the airport. They
cast shadows of the benches, of the trashcans.
People floated by in the light. It was like heaven,
a simple, boring heaven. Boring was good, it was
safe and warm.

For some time, the airport was a magical
place. I sat in a cafe', with no idea of where my
bags were, feeling as if that magic had turned
dark, and every potted plant and poster behind
glass were out to get me. It had seemed so
thrilling and fast paced. I loved it as a child.

I sat on a bench in the middle of a long
walkway of light, windows ran the span of the
walkway, looking out over the runway where golf

cart type vehicles with chains of stalls drove around the wheels of the planes, like small animals running around the feet of a larger one. On these walkways, you could move on the soft carpet, passing people, the colors of the world, as they sat and their hearts beat and small things concerned them. It felt far away from death, far into modern life, into schedules, technology, stores, books, cars. It was all things crowding the view of the singularity of death.

This was a long trip. I would end up on some distant part of the planet. The bridges of light were where I kept things together. I was away. I was safe.

Everyone around me seemed blurry, slowly phasing out. I had jumped some when I found myself dozing. I had to stay awake. Why? Because of my bags, because I had places to be. I had to stay awake because I had to. I then realized I had no idea why I had to stay awake, why I had to do anything. Everyone around me came clearly into focus, then faded. The planes outside rumbled, they pushed through the rain with their big noses; they made noise to let all know they were coming, they were leaving for the heavens. I screamed at them. Why should I care? I was happy here, in the walkway. It had all I needed. These people were no better than me. They were safe, too. I thought of nothing else but the warmth of the morning on the walkway. I liked coming into port after a long trip and to rest on the walkway with coffee. But it was not morning. It was a cold, rainy night. And I felt as if the noise of the planes would come through the walkway at anytime, taking my home away from me.

But in the morning, I knew, I would walk on paths of lights again; in the morning would come my warmth, my safe haven.

The Gilford Collection

The Death of A Sunset

It is evening in Gilford. My lorry sets back at the top of the dirt path. I have walked down the path carefully, looking at the mill in the morning sun. It is like an old masterpiece painted on life, with ragged edges and palpable history. In every brick and pane, the ignition of Gilford lives. There is little reason to worry. When they find me here my heart will have stopped. I pull out the iv in my arm and take a deep breath as my head spins. My mind goes back to when I was ten and I had nearly thrown up my birthday cake trying to hit a piñata. My brother almost busted a gut when he saw me whacking the fence with my stick, wearily asking if I was close or not. His muffled voice had sounded so indifferent on the hospital phone. That is what got me. Not that he didn't come, but that he didn't even feel bad a little bit. That indifference took something from me. When he didn't come, I felt as if someone told me I was now dying for real, as if the cancer had been a cold before, and had turned black after hearing that. Before that news, I hadn't thought much about it. So what, I am fifty. My life could have been longer, but what else did I have to do? Go on working at the docks? As far as I was concerned, the ships carried nothing in and out; I helped transfer nothing in and out, nothing at all.

I stand straight in front of the old mill's door. With a breath, I heave my foot up and kick it in. Feeling power run back into me, an excitement comes over me. I am not cured of the sickness that is nearing my brain, but for right now, I am living; for right now, this place has cured me, and I can kick in doors all day long, and no one will find me. I feel more at peace than I have for a long time. The mill looks on the inside like what you'd expect. I walk around the dusty place, rummaging through debris. I feel an excitement about possible discovery. All is possible here.

As the day wares on, I explore the mill. Around the structure, the tall grass casts shadows by the moving sun, and hugs the brick of the building under the push of the cold wind. I pull my jacket closer as I pass a broken window. It's getting colder as night comes.

In my childhood, there was this large ballroom that held school events. I would dance and things would be brighter. I felt very honest standing there, among all the others. That world seems so far now. I never thought I would get cancer. It may seem obvious, but I really didn't. I thought I would just keep living. I knew I wouldn't live forever. But who thinks of dying? I never imagined myself in a coffin, looking white on a gurney, not able to move. It all made me feel sorely sorry for myself. I wanted to cry when I saw myself in the mirror. I whispered 'poor dear' when I passed the bathroom at the hospital and saw this withered, ghostly figure staring back. I am glad to be away from mirrors.

The sun is going down. It is the death of a sunset, and I am still here. I have outlived something. I am still kicking. The future is an illusion anyway. Life happens now, not then. This is where I decide to leave. Right here, right now. By the time my body winds down, I will have already floated into the ether, to flow down a river, riding in a gondola made of clouds towards the moon. Yeah, when they find me, that is where I will be, long before my heart stops beating. The moon is bright, and the mill is old. I think, smiling, it won't be long now.

Thanks For Reading!

If you like what you've read here, feel free to head over to my blog, calebmcfarland.com, where I blog about interesting topics, and where you can also sign up to my newsletter. If you do decide to sign up, expect to recieve free samples of my upcoming books, other free stuff, as well notifications of new posts which will come with a quick summary of what they are about. I'm on Facebook and you can find me on Twitter as @CalebDMcFarland.

On the next page is the story 'Beyond The Ocean' from my upcoming short story collection of the same name. Signing up to my newsletter will get you a free sample upon its publication.

Beyond The Ocean

I breathed a satisfied breath in the small gravel courtyard. I stepped into the electric darkness, my heart felt excited as I stepped away from the trap of the inside. As I walked down the path, towards the ocean, I felt better. The ocean was a good thing. Large and simple. It made sense. Make noise, wash the sand, be an ocean. I envied the ocean. The ocean was itself. I never felt like me and I didn't knew who else I could be. I felt like I was holding place for someone else, and then I would be on my way to a place that felt right. This village didn't feel right, this life felt broken, I felt broken. But there was nothing to do, so I kept the walk going, so I kept stepping to the ocean, where greater things could be heard. The further from humanity I was, the closer to right I felt. It was like there was

something out there, beyond the ocean,
something I couldn't understand, something that
I couldn't grasp, but maybe could grasp me. I
was lost, and coming to the end of myself, and at
the end was an endless ocean, an ocean that said
nothing. So I stood at the edge of the endless blue
and listened to the talk of huge greatness. I was
small and confused, the ocean was not. At the
edge of the ocean I waited to learn something
new, when nothing came, I walked back in
silence, back to the courtyard, back to the trap.

www.ingramcontent.com/pod-product-compliance
Lightning Source LLC
Chambersburg PA
CBHW072033170626
46811CB00008B/3067